D1137306

The Multi-
Million-
Pound
Mascot

For Jan.
So she can see what she's been missing . . .

The Multi-Million-Pound Mascot

Chris Powling

Illustrated by Martin Remphrey

OXFORD
UNIVERSITY PRESS

OXFORD

UNIVERSITY PRESS

Great Clarendon Street, Oxford OX2 6DP

Oxford University Press is a department of the University of Oxford. It
furthers the University's objective of excellence in research, scholarship,
and education by publishing worldwide in

Oxford   New York
Auckland   Bangkok   Buenos Aires   Cape Town   Chennai
Dar es Salaam   Delhi   Hong Kong   Istanbul   Karachi   Kolkata
Kuala Lumpur   Madrid   Melbourne   Mexico City   Mumbai   Nairobi
São Paulo   Shanghai   Taipei   Tokyo   Toronto

Database right Oxford University Press (maker)
First published 2001
10 9 8 7 6 5 4
Printed in Great Britain

ISBN 0 19 919 382 7
Cover illustration by Martin Remphrey

Contents

CHAPTER 1

The Peanut of Power

It was a bright, blossomy Saturday towards the end of the football season . . . and there must have been magic in the air.

How else can I explain what happened?

For a start, Oldcastle Athletic – the team I've supported all my life – had just won their ninth game in a row. Now, after years in the football wilderness, we were actually on the brink of promotion to the Premier League. And what about the Cup Final next month? Under our new manager, Freddy Wedge, Oldcastle had battled its way to Wembley as well!

See what I mean?

Sheer *magic*.

No wonder our fans were wild with excitement as they streamed out of The Canyon, Oldcastle's ancient, ramshackle stadium, on that glorious April afternoon.

'WE ARE GOING UP!

WE ARE GOING UP!' they chanted.

'WE WILL WIN THE CUP!

WE WILL WIN THE CUP!' came a second chant, almost as deafening. Mind you, I bet they'd have shouted even louder if they'd known how close we all were to something really and truly magical.

I was lingering by the turnstiles at the time. As usual, Dustin, Sheena and I, along with my twin sister Mo, were deep into our post-match analysis. 'Listen, Josh,' Sheena said to me. 'Let's get this straight, OK? Oldcastle's always been a dodgy side. Can we honestly win the Cup and the title in the same season?'

'Yes!' Dustin whooped.

'We're on a roll,' I pointed out. 'A victory

roll!' And we grinned at each other triumphantly.

All except Mo, that is. Strangely, football is only a game to my sister. She can take it or leave it, she says. Maybe that's why she wasn't really listening . . . and noticed the peanut seller over by the club shop.

There he stood, a hunched-up figure dressed in brown, with a golden halo all round him from the setting sun. Even then, I remember, he seemed a bit spooky – as if he'd wandered here by accident from some forgotten, faraway place. 'Peanuts!' he called. 'Lucky peanuts!'

'*Lucky* peanuts?' said Sheena.

'Yeah, lucky if he gets rid of them,' said Dustin. 'He should be selling hot-dogs or pizza or chips. Who wants to eat peanuts you've got to shell first?'

'Me,' said Mo. Already she was rummaging in her pocket.

The peanut seller spotted her at once. In a trice, he'd shoved his tray right under her nose as he poked a grubby finger at the fat crinkly packets he hadn't sold – almost all of them from what I could see.

'Here, little lady,' he chirped. 'Any bag you care to choose. Only fifty pence to you.'

'Is that all?' Mo said.

'Cheap at half the price, my dear . . . especially as every nut in the bag comes fully laced with luck!'

'Fine,' said Mo. She picked one of the packets, slit it open straightaway and cracked a peanut out of its shell.

Suddenly, we were all staring.

Mo was holding up something between her finger and thumb. 'What's this, mister?' she said, amazed. 'A peanut shouldn't glitter like a diamond, should it?'

The peanut seller was standing very still. His brown, peanutty eyes flickered as if even he had been taken by surprise. When he spoke, his voice was awestruck . . . but with a hint of glee in it, too.

'That, little lady,' he murmured, 'is the luckiest peanut of the lot! Only one kid in a lifetime ever finds it – assuming it's found at all. What you've got there, safe and snug in your hand, is . . . is . . .'

Here, words seemed to fail him.

My sister pulled a face. 'Is *what*?' she demanded.

The peanut seller cleared his throat. 'It's known as the Peanut of Power,' he told her.

'The Peanut of Power?'

'The very same, little lady. And it belongs to you alone, its undisputed owner.'

'So what happens now?'

'You eat it,' said the peanut seller.

'Stop right there, Mo!' I snapped. 'You don't know where it's been, that nut . . .' Big mistake. When you're both the same age, eleven years and five months exactly, you don't give orders to someone as stroppy as my sister.

Instantly, she popped the nut in her mouth and swallowed it. I swear her throat seemed to sparkle from deep inside. 'Is that it, then?' she asked.

'That's it,' said the peanut seller, dreamily. 'From now on you've got luck for life – and not just ordinary luck, either. I'm talking about five-star, twenty-two carat, one hundred per cent proof good fortune of an utterly exceptional kind. You can take that for granted, my dear. Whether you deserve it or not, top quality luck will always be there for you, shifting every chance in your favour . . .'

'You're winding me up,' said Mo.

The peanut seller peered at her sharply. 'Shall I show you the sort of thing you can count on after this?' he asked.

'If you like.'

Quickly, he took Mo's fifty pence piece from his tray, flipped it high in the air and caught it in his fist as it fell. 'Call,' he invited.

'Tails,' Mo sniffed.

Tails is what it was. A fluke, obviously. Or was it?

The peanut seller flipped the coin again . . . and again. Mo's guesses were right every time. After a dozen tries in all, every one of them just as Mo predicted, Dustin, Sheena and I began to feel uneasy. 'Let *me* toss the coin,' Dustin suggested.

It didn't make the slightest difference. When Sheena and I took a turn, it was just the same. Somehow, Mo couldn't help winning.

'What's going on?' Sheena whispered. 'Is she psychic or what, Josh?'

'She's *weird*, definitely,' Dustin declared.

The peanut seller laughed. 'She's neither,' he

said. 'Simply super-lucky, that's all, just as I told you. Now you've got the Peanut of Power in your system, little lady, you can take every chance as it comes. It'll never let you down, that Peanut, in any way, shape or form.'

'Big deal,' said Mo. 'What does that make me – Queen of the coin-tossers? It's not going to change anything, is it?'

'Oh, but it might,' came a thin, foxy voice. 'Properly handled, in fact, it could be very important indeed . . .'

His words seemed to hang in the air. Goodness knows how long he'd been watching us.

Naturally, we recognized him at once.

Everyone in the city knew that oily smile, and those designer clothes, as well as his habit of mingling with the home-going fans after we'd won a match. Right now, though, his beady gaze never left my sister. 'Let's get together and talk this through,' he said smoothly.

He was Freddy Wedge, the boss of Oldcastle Athletic.

CHAPTER 2

Mo's new job

Yes, Freddy was a smooth operator all right.

He dropped a ten-pound note on the peanut seller's tray and waved him away. Then he called a mini-cab to take Dustin and Sheena home. After this, he chatted up our Gran on his mobile phone. He had her hooked from the word go. 'So you're Josh and Mo's carer, are you?' he purred. 'No parents around, then? What's that . . . you've brought them up on your own, you say?'

He clucked his tongue sympathetically when she told him about the terrible accident on the motorway, years ago, which made orphans of Mo and me. 'You're an amazing person, Mrs Nolan. Truly *amazing*,' he gushed. 'Such lovely grandchildren, too . . .'

By the time he'd finished charming her, Gran was ready to let him adopt us, practically. Not that we would have allowed it. Mo stood there, grim-faced, while he finished his call.

Later, he led us through The Canyon's scruffy corridors to his office under the main stand. Already I could feel my heart thumping with excitement about what he might have in mind for us. My sister, of course, was harder to win over.

Freddy saw he had to move fast. Quickly, he pulled open a drawer in the biggest and glossiest desk I've ever seen. He took out a brand-new pack of playing cards and a pair of dice. 'A little test,' he said silkily. 'Just to make sure we're not wasting each other's time, eh? Throw a double-six for me, will you?'

Mo picked up the dice, jiggled them in her fist, and rolled them over the desk top.

Double-six.

She threw ten more double-sixes altogether, one after the other, without a single miss – though when Freddy and I tried to do the same we got the usual random numbers.

Freddy licked his lips. 'OK,' he said. 'You're deadly with dice, then. Are you just as cute with cards?'

''Spect so,' said Mo, reluctantly. And whatever he asked for – a king, a queen, a jack – that's where she cut the deck. 'Easy-peasy,' she sniffed. 'With this luck thing of mine, somehow I can't seem to help it.'

'So I see,' said Freddy. There was a gleam in his hard, crafty eyes.

Suddenly, he pushed back his chair. 'Come next door a moment,' he invited. 'There's something I'd like to show you.' He ushered us into a small, dimly-lit lobby and switched on some spotlights. I gasped out loud.

On a huge, square table was an architect's model of the most beautiful football ground I've ever seen. It was perfect in every detail and

exactly to scale – from the seats in each towering grandstand to the tiny blades of grass on the pitch. Also it was stylish, so stylish. In such a state-of-the-art stadium, I realized, you could have played a World Cup match . . . no, more like a Universe Cup match against Mars or Venus or Jupiter. Just looking at it made me feel inter-galactic. 'Is . . . is this The Canyon?' I stammered.

'It's The Canyon of the future, son – the new home of Oldcastle Athletic.'

'When will we build it, Mr Wedge?'

'Work will begin at the end of the season, I hope – assuming everything goes right for us in our three remaining games. That's where this sister of yours comes in.'

'Me?' Mo blinked. 'What's it got to do with me? I can't play for Oldcastle Athletic.'

Freddy's long, thin face gave a twitch. 'Not *play* for us, no. We've got plenty of players on our books. What we haven't got yet . . .'

'Yes?'

'. . . is an official club *mascot*.'

'A mascot?' said Mo, innocently. 'What's a mascot?' Honestly, I could have killed her.

Instead, I gritted my teeth. 'Everyone knows what a mascot is, Mo,' I said as breezily as I could. 'It's the kid, or kids, who run onto the pitch at the start of the match and join in the kick-about before the match starts.'

'Why?' Mo asked.

'Allegedly, to bring the team luck,' said Freddy. 'It's a lot of tosh, I've always thought – a bit of showbiz to keep the crowd happy. Now, I'm not so sure.' He glanced down at his desk top. There, staring back at us, were the ace of clubs and a double-six.

When Freddy looked up again, his eyes were on me. 'We've got two league games left,' he said. 'Win those and we're champions of the First Division – with Premiership football at The Canyon next season. Also, in four weeks' time, there's Wembley . . .'

'The Cup Final,' I swallowed. 'Against Melchester United, the most famous team in the world. Can we pull off promotion *and* the Cup, Mr Wedge?'

'We're good enough, kid. And the ball's been rolling for us, no doubt about that. Just three more victories and we're home and dry with this new stadium here. It'll improve the whole area – the entire city will be back on the map, not just Oldcastle Athletic.'

'So what's the problem, then?'

'Luck, Josh – the bad kind. One slip by a player, one dud bounce of the ball, one dodgy decision by a referee and all our plans may have to be scrapped. Oldcastle Athletic haven't won a trophy for more than forty years, remember. And look what happened the last time we did . . .'

I bit my lip. Everyone in the city knew about Oldcastle's one-and-only trophy. It had disappeared completely soon after it was first presented. 'Mislaid during ground improvements,' was the official explanation but no one really knew where it went. It was one of the great mysteries of football. Some people said Oldcastle Athletic had never recovered from the loss.

Maybe my sister could change that . . .

Freddy seemed to think so, anyway. He turned to Mo, his voice suddenly smarmy. 'So what's your opinion, girlie?' he asked. 'Are you up to the job, d'you reckon?'

Girlie?

I wasn't a bit surprised by Mo's reply. Immediately, she went into a full-facial scowl. 'I'm not being anyone's mascot,' she mumbled.

'If *I* say you are — '

'No!'

'Mr Wedge!' I exclaimed. But it was too late. CRACK! His fist had thudded on the tabletop so heavily we saw The

Canyon
of the future
shudder from end to end
as if from an earthquake.

This was enough for my sister. For a moment she simply stared at him. Her lip curled in disgust as if he were something nasty you had to scrape off your shoe. Then, abruptly, she turned away. Already she was reaching for the paperback in her hip pocket. We heard Freddy's door click shut behind her and her footsteps fading along the corridor in no particular hurry at all. Freddy glared at me. 'Where's she's gone?' he snarled.

'Somewhere private, Mr Wedge – until she's calmed down. She'll read her book until she's in a good mood again.'

'Good mood, eh? I'll give her good mood . . . what that kid needs is a good hiding.'

'And what you need is a mascot,' I said.

I'd pitched my voice just right. Freddy's eyes narrowed. I could almost see his brain balancing the possibilities as he weighed up what Mo had to offer against the fuss and bother she'd bring. Then his gaze drifted back to the gorgeous stadium-in-waiting in front of us. Casually, he reached over the soaring grandstands and flicked a speck of dust off one of the penalty spots.

That's when I knew for sure that my sister hadn't quite blown her chances.

CHAPTER 3

Up for the Cup

I had an hour to get Mo sorted, no more. After that, he'd offer the job of mascot to some other kid or dump the idea altogether.

That's what Freddy said, anyway.

As he steered me out of his office, I couldn't help noticing there was still a glint in the manager's eye. Where should I start searching, though? In a cranky, old-fashioned place like The Canyon I could imagine a hundred different hideaways for a kid who wanted to bury herself in a book. 'Don't panic, Josh,' I told myself. 'She can't be far.'

I searched pretty thoroughly. I shoved my head in cupboards full of old match programmes, in a room cluttered with gleaming keep-fit equipment, even in a walk-in closet where shelf after shelf was stacked high with shirts and shorts and socks – all piled pretty haphazardly it seemed to me.

Then I saw the tunnel. It sloped upwards with a glimpse of sky at the far end. Knowing exactly where it led, I couldn't resist tucking a make-believe ball under my arm and breaking into a trot till I burst out in the open air. There, across a cinder track, was the pitch itself – a touch threadbare in places at this stage of the season, but still cropped to a snooker table smoothness. I could hear the snap of the wind in the corner flags and the rustle of netting behind each goal.

OK, so the thrill of it sent me stupid. Tipping back my head, I let rip with the latest Oldcastle anthem:

Our back four are killers –
Smith, Tate, Tarbo and Spillers!

Our midfield is brainy –
Ben Vronsky and Rainey!
Our forwards are deadly –
Okri, Dent, Neame and Headley!
And in goal we've got Racer Carr –
So we'll smash you, whoever you are!

It sounded great to me . . . until I realized I could hear a second voice echoing every word I sang.

Was The Canyon haunted? Slowly, my stomach quaking, I turned around. My singing partner was sitting in the dug-out beside the tunnel. He was so small, he'd have looked much the same age as me if it weren't for his wrinkled, weather-beaten face and shock of dazzling white hair. 'Hi, kid,' he said, giving me a wave.

'Hi,' I managed to wave back. I didn't need to ask his name. He was as famous as the faded tracksuit he wore and the crumpled carrier bag he held in his lap. 'Hi, Uncle Patch!' I added hoarsely.

'That's one–nil to you, son. Now, kindly

allow me to equalize by passing on your name.'

'I'm Josh – Josh Nolan. I'm here with my twin sister, Mo. Mr Wedge might make her the club's new mascot.'

'Lucky, is she?'

'You could say that . . .' And I found myself telling Oldcastle's trainer the whole story.

Uncle Patch lifted an eyebrow when I'd finished. 'A *peanut* seller?' he frowned. 'I haven't seen one of those at The Canyon in years – not since I was a kid myself, in fact. As for this Peanut of Power business, all I can say is that it sounds to me more like a fairy story than football. Mind you, if Foxy Freddy's on the case there's got to be something in it. Never misses a trick, that man.

'Speaking for myself, I'd rather we took our luck as it comes whether it's good or bad. But that sort of opinion gets you shown a red card nowadays. Winning at all costs seems to be the only strategy that counts.'

'Don't you want Oldcastle to be champions, then?' I asked. 'And maybe win the Cup as well?'

The old trainer stared at me as if I'd gone mad. For a while he didn't answer. Eventually, as if breaking a spell, he shook his Santa Claus hair so hard it stuck out more crazily then ever. 'Champions?' he said wistfully. 'And Cup-winners? Josh, that's what I dream about every night. I've been treating cuts, bruises, breakages, cramp, concussion, torn ligaments and plain disappointment for more than forty years on this pitch . . . and the closest I've ever come to handling any silverware is polishing the knives and forks in the directors' dining room. In all that time, the club's only picked up a single, solitary trophy . . . which was such a shock it went walkabout straightaway and has never been seen since. Heard about that little disaster, have you?'

'Hasn't everyone?'

'Fair comment,' he agreed. 'Believe me, Josh, if Oldcastle could shake off the habit of a lifetime and actually *win* something before I'm carried off on my final stretcher . . .' Uncle Patch broke off with a sigh.

I sighed, too. Right now, most of the city had its fingers crossed for Oldcastle. Meanwhile, the kid who didn't have to cross her fingers at all was nowhere to be found.

Or was she?

Suddenly, a light went on in my brain. 'Uncle Patch?' I said. 'Is there a window to read by in that closet where all the team strip is kept?'

'What's that, Josh? Now you come to mention it, there *is* a window in the far corner . . .'

And so there was.

Mo had kept herself out of sight, of course, by piling clean laundry all round her – which was why the kit had looked so untidy to me. 'Hi, Josh,' she yawned from the farthest shelf. 'Have you finished with His Royal Freddiness already? I hope you talked him out of this mascot rubbish.'

'Rubbish?' I said. 'Why is it rubbish, Mo? It might make all the difference to Oldcastle. Ask Uncle Patch here. He's been the club's trainer for years.'

'True enough,' nodded Uncle Patch. 'And I stopped being surprised by anything in football years ago. What's so wrong with being a mascot, anyway? Most kids jump at the chance – some clubs even charge their parents for the privilege. Yet here you're being offered the job for nothing, Mo. You'd be Oldcastle's official mascot for three key matches. How come you're so set against the idea?'

'Because it's so show-offy . . . I'd have to prance about in front of thousands of people. They'd all be staring at me.'

Uncle Patch scratched his head. 'Well, I can't deny that. A mascot's got to be there in the actual stadium, I admit – preferably making her presence felt out on the pitch. That goes without saying, I'm afraid.'

'Then it's not for me.'

'So why not split the job with your twin, here? Let Josh do all the crowd-pleasing stuff while you sit back in the stands where no one will notice you – except you'll be bringing us the actual luck.'

I gaped at the old trainer, stunned. 'Will that really work, Uncle Patch?'

'Don't see why not. Plenty of teams have more than one mascot, after all. That's the norm, in fact. So why shouldn't Oldcastle have a couple, one secret and one up-front?'

'Mo, how does that sound to you?'

My sister eyed me shrewdly. She could tell how much this meant to me and she was wavering. So I bit my lip to tip the odds my way.

Now she was hooked. '*Three* matches?' she said.

'That's all, I promise.'

'And after that it'll all be over?'

'Trust me,' I begged.

'OK, then.'

'*Yes!*' I punched the air with relief.

Mo, meanwhile, had slid off the shelf where she'd been lying and slipped her paperback into her pocket. She had something else in her hands, too – a bulky object wrapped up in an ancient Oldcastle shirt. 'What have you got there, Mo?' asked Uncle Patch.

'Don't know,' she shrugged. 'It was stuck at the back there. It looks like it fell down that gap in the shelving.'

'Yes, but what *is* it?'

'Haven't looked.' She unravelled the shirt to see.

CLUNK!

Mo's object hit the floor with a dull, metallic thud. Slowly, it rolled over the floor towards Uncle Patch and me. It was a cup, shaped somewhere between a goblet and a flower vase, rather old-fashioned by today's standards but still shiny between its dark smears of tarnish.

All three of us were struck dumb. Uncle Patch was the first to react. He sank to his knees like a knight in the olden days who's found the Holy Grail. 'You realize what this is, don't you?' he whispered. 'It's the only trophy Oldcastle has ever won. Forty-three years it's been missing – since this grandstand was first built. Everyone thought it was buried or stolen. Yet here it's been all along till . . . till . . .'

'Till Mo got lucky,' I said.

CHAPTER 4

Our first fixture

The goal that made Mo and me famous came when . . . no. Hold on, Josh. You're getting ahead of yourself here. Actually, Oldcastle Athletic's new mascot was famous before a ball had even been kicked.

Nothing else had been happening, I suppose – what journalists call a 'slow' news day. Because suddenly, to everyone's surprise, just about every sports writer in the land descended on The Canyon to find out about the kid who'd discovered the club's long-lost trophy.

Freddy was delighted, of course. 'Keep 'em

guessing' was his motto. He set up a series of press releases, interviews and photo-shoots that raised far more questions than they answered. Soon the reporters were hopping up and down with frustration. 'But who *is* this mascot, Freddy?' they demanded.

'Just a kid . . . a kid with a special talent. A *very* special talent, to be honest, thanks to the Peanut of Power.'

'Oh, yes . . . the magical peanut. Nice touch that, Freddy. Tell us his name, though. Or is it *her* name? That's what everyone wants to know.'

'Later,' Freddy insisted.

'But you said that last time.'

'And I'll say it next time, as well . . . or will I?' Here, he seemed tempted to go on. No wonder they came back for more.

Even Uncle Patch was impressed. 'Foxy Freddy may be as bent as a blinkin' banana shot,' he admitted, 'but he's a kind of genius when it comes to drumming up publicity.'

Altogether, Oldcastle's boss made absolutely

certain that our next match was a sell-out. Also, maybe, a dogfight.

It was an away-game, you see – a local derby against our neighbouring club, Binborough Rovers. Binborough weren't at all pleased about the fuss Freddy had been causing, especially when he announced that his new mascot would be sitting on the touchline to bring Athletic all the luck going but wouldn't actually run onto the pitch to greet the crowd. 'We're saving that till next week,' he said, loftily. 'When we're playing at home.'

'What an insult,' Uncle Patch groaned. 'Binborough have had a pretty iffy season compared with us . . . but now they're so furious they'll want to bury us.'

'Mo won't let them,' I said uneasily.

'You reckon?'

The old trainer glanced towards the visitor's enclosure where Mo, in full Oldcastle regalia just like me, was sitting between Dustin and Sheena. Could she really work her luck from there? I shut my eyes tight and huddled in a corner of the dug-out so the fans would have a hard time spotting me. To my relief, Oldcastle won the toss and kicked off.

At this point, I'd love to give a ball-by-ball account of the game. The trouble is, I can't. For the next couple of hours I simply slumped on the bench in a jittery heap, like a zombie in green-and-gold football gear with a green-and-gold painted face.

'Stage-fright,' was Uncle Patch's explanation. 'Lots of people get it with their first appearance in front of a crowd as big as this.'

All afternoon, though?

I felt a complete idiot, I can tell you. It was the following day, in Gran's sitting room, before I really found out what had happened. Dustin had videoed the match for us from his dad's sports channel. 'Where's Mo?' he said.

'She's out in the kitchen,' I said, 'working on some kind of experiment.' They stared at me in disbelief.

I tried to explain. 'It's her latest thing.' I told them. 'She's gone dead keen on science stuff.'

Being twins and looking so similar, Mo and I had discovered long ago that people expected us to be the same in every other way as well. This may be true of identical twins but not fraternal twins like us. Our reaction to Mum and Dad's accident showed this. I went a bit mad for months, especially at school. Mo, on the other hand, had gone very quiet. You never saw her without her nose in a book. Hadn't Dustin and Sheena noticed this at the time? They were our best friends, after all.

Dustin chuckled and reached for the remote

control. 'Who cares? She's the best mascot Oldcastle have ever had. Shall we go straight to the winning goal?'

'Yeah!' I agreed. Up came the pictures and commentary.

Astonishingly, the scorer was our keeper and captain Racer Carr – so-called for his speed in closing down a shooting-angle or snapping up a loose cross. 'Stalemate, then,' said the voice-over just before Racer clinched it. 'Only sixty seconds left after eighty-nine minutes of edgy, negative play in which neither side has taken a chance on anything. What a wash-out! And Oldcastle's much-publicized new mascot hasn't been much help to them . . .'

'Famous last words!' Sheena giggled.

'Shush!' hissed Dustin. 'Here comes the funniest foul-up in the whole history of football!' It was, too.

Tall and gangly, Racer had hit a long clearance from his own penalty area. Suddenly, a freak gust of wind carried the ball higher and higher upfield. The Binborough keeper was caught out of position – and spotted the danger much too late. As he scuttled desperately backwards, he lost his footing and was propelled into a perfect head-over-heels in reverse . . . just as the ball, with perfect timing,

bounced neatly off the seat of his pants into the empty net behind him. 'Bum–nil!' howled the commentator. 'Er . . . one–nil is what I mean.'

Poor goalie. The home fans didn't know whether to laugh or cry. This wasn't a problem for Dustin, Sheena and me in Granny's sitting room, you can bet. We nearly wet ourselves as we watched. Our laughs lasted most of the day, in fact – through four viewings of the entire match as well as umpteen repeats of Racer's hilarious winning goal.

In all that time, Mo didn't enter the room even once.

CHAPTER 5

Everything to gain

Can you be crushed by a landslide of sound? I nearly was. The instant I stepped on the pitch, a week later, the whole of The Canyon seemed to collapse on me in one vast, lung-bursting roar. I felt like a small flickering candle on a birthday cake with twenty thousand mouths trying to blow me out . . . every one of them making a wish. Already the chanting had begun.

JOSH! JOSH! JOSH! JOSH!

NO-LAN! NO-LAN! NO-LAN!

My name, yes.

Following the Binborough match, Freddy had announced who I was on television. To be fair, he'd checked this with Gran first. 'It's simple, Mrs Nolan,' he told her. 'Josh will have hundreds and thousands of unofficial security guards in every corner of the city. The Press, or anyone else, won't get anywhere near him.'

'If you say so, Mr Wedge,' said Gran doubtfully. But he was quite right.

Now they had an actual kid to relate to – a living, breathing person, not some anonymous peanut-eater – the fans took me to their hearts. It was like being surrounded by guardian angels wherever I went. Even in school I was treated with a polite, smiling respect. And that was just the teachers. Of course, we kept it secret that Oldcastle's real mascot was my twin sister, Mo.

So, despite all the fuss, there was no stage fright this time. Having met the first team squad, attended a couple of training sessions and even signed a few autographs outside the ground, I'd got my nerves well under control. I felt really great as I strutted my stuff round The Canyon's touchline with Oldcastle's long lost cup held high above my head. 'Meet the lad with the luck, fans!' the sound system boomed. 'It's our own – our very own – *JOSH NOOOO-LAN!*'

The crowd picked up on it at once.

JOSH NOOOO-LAN!

JOSH NOOOO-LAN!

JOSH NOOOO-LAN!

Honestly, it was so cool.

When, eventually, our players appeared to the sort of welcome most teams only dream about, Uncle Patch shook his snowy head in admiration. 'Well done, Josh!' he greeted me as I sat down on the bench beside him. 'That was quite a performance.' I thought so, too.

Mind you, it needed to be. This wasn't just our final league match of the season. After our three points against Binborough, a win today would make us First Division Champions.

At last the game began. Our opponents, Hudwich Albion, were hovering halfway up the table so they had nothing to lose just as we had everything to gain. Maybe that's why the football was inspired from the very first peep of the referee's whistle. 'Immaculate,' I heard Uncle Patch mutter to himself over and over again. 'Absolutely immaculate.' At no point did luck get a look in.

By half-time, the score was one–all. Both goals had been technically flawless, giving neither keeper a chance. In the dressing-room the players clamoured for our trainer's opinion. 'Got any advice for us, Uncle?' they demanded.

'It's anybody's game, lads. Also it's a *great* game, so don't change a thing.'

'How about you, Josh?' grinned Racer Carr.

'Yeah,' added the two Bens, Vronsky and Rainey, who seemed to do everything in unison. 'Got a nifty bit of Nolanry up your sleeve for after the interval?'

'Er . . . such as what?' I asked.

Jeff Okri, our leading scorer and resident comedian, snapped his fingers. 'How about a handy dollop of bird-pooh in my marker's eye?' he suggested. 'You know, just when I've got the goal gaping in front of me.'

Everyone laughed. I did my best to join in, naturally. How could I tell them it was all down to my sister, not me? As usual, Uncle Patch came to my rescue. 'Just play, lads,' he interrupted. 'Play your hearts out and hope for the best result of the lot – the one you truly deserve.'

'Good thinking, Uncle,' Racer nodded. The others mumbled their agreement.

The second half turned out to be even more exciting than the first. Slowly, the score crept up to three–three. All four goals – like those before them – were unstoppable. Two came from set-pieces just outside the area and the others, one for either side, from individual bits of wizardry.

Again, there seemed no room left for mere luck. Given the fierce pace of play and the knife-edge balance between the two sides, probably most of the Oldcastle fans had forgotten their mascot altogether. They soon had a reminder, though.

In a way, I suppose, the Hudwich players can only blame themselves for what happened in the last, hushed minute of the match. They had heard about Binborough Rovers, after all. So when Jeff Okri, out on the wing, swung that final hopeful cross towards the Albion goal they should have been ready for anything. Here's what they weren't ready for: *JOSH NOOOO-LAN!*

Was it an echo? Or some stray gust of wind trapped in The Canyon's antiquated grandstands? Wherever it came from, what surprised us was the sudden spooky howl right at this particular moment.

JOSH NOOOO-LAN! Instantly, we all took our eyes off the ball.

This meant that no one, literally no one – not the goalkeeper, not the referee, not even Jeff Okri himself – saw the ball drift gently into the furthest corner of the Hudwich net.

GOAL! My sister's luck had struck again.

Naturally, our fans went berserk. This noise

wasn't a mere landslide – more like a volcano erupting. Krakatoa itself, exploding over the South Seas, couldn't have been any louder. 'We've done it!' I screeched through the hubbub. 'Uncle Patch, we've really and truly done it! That's four–three to us . . . we're top of the table! We're Champions of the First Division!

'So we are,' said Uncle Patch gruffly. He said something like that, anyway. Actually, he was so busy blowing his nose into a huge, green-and-gold handkerchief, he could have been crying his eyes out for all I could see.

CHAPTER 6

The multi-million-pound mascot

Freddy's plans for the fortnight run-up till Wembley took me completely by surprise. 'Do nothing,' he advised.

'Nothing, Mr Wedge?'

'Nothing at all, son. Of course, we'll coach you for the day itself. Otherwise, just rest. That goes for your sister, too.'

'He's right, you know,' said Uncle Patch. 'This mascot business has been more of a strain than you realize. Get some peace and quiet while you can, Josh. Foxy Freddy will sort things out with your headteacher, I'm sure.'

'If that's what you think,' I shrugged. And suddenly I longed for a break myself. Mostly, I dozed in an armchair or mooched around the house getting in Gran's way. Sometimes, though, I'd sit hunched at my bedroom window gazing out at the waterfront . . . or what was left of the waterfront. These days, it was a wasteland of empty warehouses flanked by rusting, heavy-duty machinery. Even the sea, where I glimpsed it, had a lifeless out-of-work look. But wouldn't all this be transformed, too, along with the rest of the city, if Freddy managed to build The Canyon of the future?

My sister, needless to say, was quieter than ever. We'd always shared things, discussing our problems endlessly, but somehow neither of us wanted to mention her marvellous luck. We didn't even mention Oldcastle's chances. I still wasn't convinced that they could win against Melchester United.

Some people believed it, though. One of them was Freddy Wedge – or so he said on

53

Soccer Special. This was a late-night TV programme on the eve of Cup Final day. I'd persuaded Gran to let Mo and me watch it while she was upstairs fussing over our packing for London. Mo lay back on the sofa, already half-asleep.

Me, I was riveted. Especially when Freddy leant forward in his chair and tapped Melchester United's manager on the knee. 'Alex,' he said. 'How much is a top-grade striker worth to a football team?'

'The best there is, you mean?'

'Exactly.'

'Millions of pounds, I'd say . . . multi-millions, in fact. A striker of that quality would be priceless.'

'So what does a striker do that makes him so valuable?'

The Melchester manager stared at him as if he'd gone barmy. 'He scores goals, Freddy. Everyone knows that.'

'In every match?'

'Sorry?'

'Does the best international striker score in every match, Alex? A goal-a-game, would you say?'

'Not in every match, no. There's never been a striker in the whole of footballing history who can guarantee a goal-a-game. Why, Freddy? D'you think you've got someone like that?'

'Not a striker, no.'

At this point, Freddy sat back in his chair. 'I've got a mascot like that, though,' he smirked. 'So far, thanks to the Peanut of Power, we've had a goal a game out of Josh Nolan . . . which, in my book, must make him the world's first ever Multi-Million-Pound Mascot!' Here, right on cue, came a clip of the bum-nil incident at Binborough shown in slow-motion as usual. This dissolved straightaway into *JOSH NOOOO-LAN!* . . . and Jeff Okri's last-gasp cross from the wing which destroyed Hudwich Albion.

The programme finished with a close-up of a peanut – a fat, crunchy-looking peanut – which glistened like a diamond as the camera zoomed in on it.

As a piece of psyching-out it was brilliant. How Freddy persuaded the television people to co-operate, I'll never know. Maybe he really was a genius. Then again, maybe he'd just made the biggest mistake of his life. My sister, you see, had swung her legs off the sofa and was sitting bolt upright with her eyes fixed on the screen.

Clearly, she'd heard every word.

CHAPTER 7

Injury time

The trip to London was arranged by Freddy personally. He'd hired a Rolls Royce for himself and Granny – taking Dustin and Sheena along, too. Their job was to sit in the front seat, beside the chauffeur, dressed from top to toe in the club's colours. 'You'll be in a different car,' he explained to Mo and me. 'Your friends are just a decoy.'

'A decoy?' I frowned.

Freddy smiled his foxiest smile. 'Only a precaution, son. Half the Press in the country will be after you for an interview. So we'll lead

them to an entirely different hotel. It's
nowhere near where you'll be staying.'

'Suppose they still find us, Mr Wedge?'

'Higgins will sort it.'

One glance at big, brawny Mr Higgins –
Freddy's minder – told me how good he'd be at
sorting it. He was good at driving, too. I'd have
loved every minute of our journey south in the
dark, low-slung sports car if Mo hadn't been so
quiet all the
way.

What was
the matter
with her?

Her face wore
what Granny used
to call her mess-
and-stomp-in-it
look. Not that I
could see very
much of her
face. Mostly,
she kept her

head stuck in whatever it was she was reading. 'That car's breaking the speed limit, Mo!' I remember pointing out. Or, 'Almost there, Mo!'

She ignored everything I said to her.

Our hotel was tucked away in a side-street of quiet, solid houses which seemed designed to attract no attention to themselves. It felt utterly safe, I admit. According to the brochure I picked up in the lobby, every room was sound-proof, thief-proof, fire-proof – also, for all I knew, guest-proof as well, since no one else seemed to have signed in. Had Freddy booked the whole place for us? Even our sour, softly-spoken landlady was like some kind of warder.

After we'd finished supper in our own private dining-room, Mr Higgins sat back in his chair. 'How about an early night, kids?' he suggested. 'You've got a big day ahead of you, tomorrow.'

'Brilliant,' said Mo, sleepily. 'Just what I fancy.'

'Me, too,' I said.

Now I was really worried. Since when had

Mo ever opted to go to bed early, however tired she was?

So, up in my sound-proof, thief-proof, fire-proof room, I left my door a little bit open. And I lay down fully-dressed in the dark. If I knew Mo, she wouldn't keep me waiting long. Just before midnight she made her move.

At first I almost missed it – the faintest possible rattle of the iron bar spanning the emergency exit at the end of the corridor.

Where was my sister going? And what would she do when she got there . . .

mess and stomp in it?

Cautiously, slinky as a spy, I

followed at a safe distance down the

fire escape and out into the street. At the corner of the main road, I slipped into the shadows just before she glanced back the way she'd come. She'd halted by one of those big containers where grit and rock-salt are stored for spreading over an icy road. It was probably full to the brim after last month's unexpected snowstorm.

She seemed to be testing the container's weight. It was much too heavy to be budged. By an eleven-year-old, anyway. But not by the huge bag-lady who appeared from a doorway just when Mo needed her. I saw Mo saying something. She pointed at the container. 'Sis, what *are* you up to?' I muttered.

Vandalism, that's what. The bag-lady nodded, spat on a pair of hands the size of shovels and braced herself against the container. With one heave she'd overturned it – sending a cascade of grit and rock-salt slithering across the road surface where it glittered in the lamplight from one kerb to the other. I watched, baffled, as my sister waved the bag-lady goodbye.

Had she gone mad? Mo's next step seemed to confirm her nuttiness. Ahead of us was a stretch of pavement which had been opened up for repairs. Of course, it was cordoned off with the usual fences, flashing lights and warning signs. Mo took no notice of these. She clambered over the barriers, dropped down into the trench and marched straight along it – stomp – stomp – stomp – scuffing up muck and dust as she went.

'Stop!' I cried hoarsely. 'Mo —'

'Hey, you!' came a roar from the end of the street. 'Did you do this? And why are you down that hole?' A policeman, up to his ankles in rock-salt, had seen her.

By now Mo was back on the pavement and running, you can bet. So was I. We had a flying start, thank goodness. In fact, we'd have got clean away if Mo hadn't suddenly pulled up.

We stood there, panting, in front of one of the vastest shop-windows I've ever seen. Every detail of me, my twin sister and the midnight

street behind us was reflected in its smooth, polished glass. Mo stooped for a chunk of paving-stone. 'This'll do,' she said.

'No,' I yelled. 'Don't even think —'

But she'd thrown it already.

As you'd expect with her kind of luck, she hit the glass dead-centre. The jangling, ear-splitting crash as the entire window shattered in front of us was like the biggest chandelier in the world hitting the hardest ballroom floor. Mo grinned a bit shakily. 'OK, Josh,' she said. 'We'd better get out of here.'

'Really?' I snarled. 'I can't think why.' Already I could hear the approach of heavy, big-booted feet.

Grabbing Mo's arm so hard I almost wrenched it out of its socket, I yanked her after me into the darkness.

CHAPTER 8

Mo blows the whistle

Sheer panic kept us running flat out. It also helped being city kids – even if this wasn't our city. Mo and I were well used to byways, back alleys and the sort of dead-end which isn't, especially at night, if you're prepared to take a risk. I didn't let us slow down till the stitch in my side felt like major surgery. 'This is far enough,' I wheezed. 'That cop must be miles away by now.'

'Where are we, Josh?'

'No idea.' Heaving for breath, I stared around us.

Bit by bit, from the rustle of the yew trees overhead and the glimmer of moonlight on stonework, I began to get a sense of the place. 'It's a graveyard, I think . . . yes, see that church-like shape over there? You can just make out the front porch!'

'It's spooky, Josh.'

'Spooky?' I said icily. 'It's nothing like as spooky as the stunts you've been pulling tonight. Have you gone completely off your head, Mo?'

She let me drag her into the church porch where we slumped on a bench too dark to be visible. I was still trembling with anger. This made Mo's quietness even more infuriating. When she spoke, she almost sounded proud of herself.

'I'm sorry, Josh,' she said. 'But I had to do it.'

'Had to do *what*?' I snapped.

I felt Mo look at me. 'Haven't you worked out yet what I've been up to?'

'Tell me . . .' I growled.

'I've been dumping my luck.'

I felt a sudden stab of alarm.

Mo's fingers fluttered on my shoulder. 'Think about it, Josh. If you're lumbered with unbelievable luck like me, how do you get back to being normal again? You try the opposite of all that rabbit's-foot and four-leaf clover rubbish, don't you? What I needed was *bad* luck to take away the power of the Peanut.'

'To take it *away*?' I said.

'So I spilt some salt – the biggest batch of salt I could find. And I stepped on a humungous crack in the pavement. As for breaking a mirror, I reckon that shop window's got to be worth *seventy* years bad luck, never mind seven!'

'More like seven hundred,' I groaned. 'Mo, I know this mascot business isn't easy. It's the same for me, remember, only I'm not the one with the luck. You are. Couldn't you put up with it just a little longer? There's only one match to play, after all!'

'You've got me all wrong, Josh,' said my sister. 'I *do* want Oldcastle to win. Not as much as you, maybe, but I really do. Who wouldn't, when it means so much for the city? You heard what Freddy said on television, though. "The Multi-Million-Pound Mascot" is what he called me. "Worth a goal a game," he reckoned. If Oldcastle win today he'll *never* let me retire, not ever . . . and even if he did, other teams would be falling over themselves to get hold of me. And I don't mean just footballers, either. It could be rugby-players or cricketers or golfers . . . just about anyone who's keen to grab all the luck that's going. I'll be stuck as a mascot *forever.*'

'Mo . . .'

'Just listen to me for once, Josh. Becoming a celebrity has changed you. We don't get on, do we, like we used to? You can't think about anything except Oldcastle and winning.' She went on more quickly. 'All I can think about is my luck – that, really, it's a kind of cheating.'

'Cheating?' I said.

'It's a rip-off, Josh. It's great for *our* team, yes. But how would you like it if Binborough had been the lucky ones? Or Hudwich? Or Melchester in the Final? What d'you think they feel about Oldcastle's mascot?'

I hadn't thought about it that way. 'Mo, you mean . . .'

'Why is it OK for *us* to have all the luck? It's exactly like cheating, isn't it? Answer me, Josh.'

The trouble was, I couldn't. Nor could I help remembering what Uncle Patch had said. About taking your chances as they come, whether they're good or bad. About the best result of the lot being the one you truly deserve. Stuff like that.

We stayed there for

ages, talking it over. Eventually, I felt my sister's hand close over mine in that pitch-black, bum-freezing porch. She had a catch in her throat as she spoke. 'Josh . . .' she began.

'Yes?'

'Do you know what really bugs me about this luck of mine?'

'Tell me, Mo.' But I think I knew already.

Mo's voice seemed to hang in the darkness. 'Why wasn't I lucky when we really needed it, Josh? When Mum and Dad were on that motorway, for instance.'

It was a good question. But neither of us knew the answer.

'OK, Mo,' I said at last. 'Somehow we'll muddle through this just like we did last time. Let's get back to the hotel before Mr Higgins notices we're missing.'

'Thanks, Josh.' Suddenly, she sounded like an ordinary eleven-year-old again.

As for me, struggling to keep my mind off the game at Wembley, I felt about one hundred and eleven. But the excitement wasn't over yet.

Once we'd groped our way through the graveyard as far as the church gates, we stopped dead in our tracks. Evidently, the police hadn't been that far behind.

There were four of them altogether: a speed-cop straddling a motorbike, a couple of constables leaning on their panda-car and the patrol officer who'd spotted Mo's antics earlier, his boots and trousers still caked with rock-salt. His eyes widened with recognition. 'There they are, Sarge!' he exclaimed, pointing. 'I was certain they'd be round here somewhere.'

'Good work,' said the sergeant. With an agonizing slowness, he dismounted from his motorbike.

Just as slowly, he removed his helmet and gloves.

Then he flipped open a notebook, pencil poised. 'Are you Josh Nolan?' he asked. 'The famous mascot?'

'That's right,' I nodded, biting my lip.

'So who's your friend here?'

'This is Mo, my twin sister. She's … she's …

well, I suppose she's my assistant, sort of.'

'See?' said the sergeant to the others. 'Didn't I tell you that was the explanation?' When he turned back to us, he was beaming with delight. 'Who else but a kid like Josh Nolan would have smothered a dangerous pool of diesel oil with rock-salt?'

'Diesel oil?' I frowned.

'It was flooding the street, Josh. Not any more, though. No gas leak down in the roadworks, either, once you'd given us the tip-off!'

'What gas leak?' I asked, faintly.

'Then, to cap it all, you cracked that shop window wide open so we had a perfect view of the burglars stealing the safety-deposit boxes inside! Stopped a major robbery, you did – alongside preventing a couple of potentially horrendous accidents. Not bad for one night's work!

'Look,' I protested. 'I didn't know about any of this.'

The sergeant stopped me with a wagging finger. 'Maybe you didn't, Josh. But, thanks to you, each incident was drawn to our attention. What were you really up to, lad? Letting off steam before the big match? Well, it's lucky for us you did. This is the best night's policing we've ever had on this patch. And it's all down to you, son. Er . . . would you do us one last favour?'

'Sure,' I swallowed.

'Will you autograph this notebook, please? So we can prove it was really you who helped us?'

'No problem,' I managed to say. I scribbled my name on the page and dated it. In return, they bundled us into the panda car and gave us a lift back to our hotel.

All the way there, the driver chattered on and on about Oldcastle's prospects – sky-high, according to him, with me on the bench. I replied as cagily as I could. Mo, though, never uttered a word. Every so often, when the panda car swept under some streetlights or was lit by a passing traffic signal, I caught a glimpse of her face staring dry-eyed into the night. She looked as blank and stricken as a home supporter when the other side have scored.

I knew how that felt all right.

CHAPTER 9

Pre-match planning

For the rest of the night I lay awake, worrying. No, not worrying exactly. To be honest, I'd worked out what I needed to do even before I got into bed. What made me toss and turn for hours was deciding if I was tough enough, and clever enough, to see it through.

Did I have any choice, though?

By the time a thin, watery sun had risen over the rooftops of West London, I'd made up my mind. I bathed, dressed and slipped into Mo's room to check her out. She was sound asleep still, her face so pale and expressionless on the pillow she looked like a ghost of herself worn out with haunting. While I was there, she didn't stir even once.

So far, so good then.

Downstairs, in the dining room, I got just the answer I wanted when our steely, low-voiced landlady served me my breakfast. 'After you've gone,' she said, 'I'll be closing the place straightaway, Josh. Cleaning up can wait till tomorrow. That nice Mr Wedge has given me a ticket for the match . . . so I'm treating myself to a tip-top lunch in someone else's hotel for a change.'

'Enjoy yourself,' I smiled.

She smiled back at me, frostily. 'That's certainly my intention, young man. Will you let me know when you're ready to leave?'

I promised it wouldn't be long. After that I had to get a move on. Up in my room again, I crossed my fingers and picked up the phone. First I spoke to Gran – not easy with Dustin and Sheena jabbering in the background – then to Freddy Wedge himself. After this, I phoned Mr

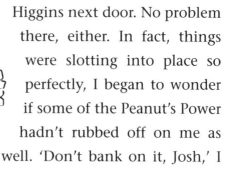

Higgins next door. No problem there, either. In fact, things were slotting into place so perfectly, I began to wonder if some of the Peanut's Power hadn't rubbed off on me as well. 'Don't bank on it, Josh,' I muttered. 'Your next call is the trickiest of the lot.' I tapped in the number.

Mo took ages to answer. 'Gran?' she said eventually, her voice still bleary with sleep.

'It's me, Mo. I'm phoning from my room.'

'Josh?'

'Don't worry, nothing's wrong. There's been a last-minute change of plan, that's all. Mo, there's food and drink in the fridge over by the window. And I've left some comics on your bedside table in case you get fed up with your book. If you like, you can even watch the match on television.'

'On television?'

'That's what I said, yes.'

I could almost hear her wrestling herself awake. 'But why would I do that, Josh?' she yawned. 'I'll be there in the stadium, won't I?'

'Ah . . .' I said. 'That's where the change of plan comes in. You won't be visiting Wembley after all, Mo. This afternoon I'm going to the Cup Final on my own.'

'On your own?'

'Of course, no one else will know that – just the two of us. Gran, Dustin and Sheena think you'll be down in the dugout with me . . . and Freddy thinks you'll be up in the grandstand with them. As for Mr Higgins, he thinks you've left for the ground already.'

'I don't get it, Josh.'

'Don't you?'

I paused to let her gather her thoughts.

Then continued before she could interrupt. 'It's really quite simple, Mo. If everyone assumes you're there at Wembley and Oldcastle go on to lose . . . it'll be obvious you've finally run out of luck.'

'But what if Oldcastle win?'

'Without you, Mo? A mascot can't influence the game from outside the ground. That's what Uncle Patch reckoned, anyway. So they'd have to win on merit.'

'Well . . . it's possible, isn't it?'

I laughed. 'Just about possible, yes. That's beside the point, though. At least if you're stashed away here at the hotel it can't be a *lucky* win. It'll be a normal football match with luck on both sides. When people see that, all this fuss about The Peanut of Power will fade away. It'll look like a typical Freddy Wedge publicity stunt.'

'So it doesn't matter if Oldcastle win or lose?'

'Exactly,' I said. 'Either way, your career as a mascot will be over. And another thing, Mo . . .'

'Yes?'

' . . . it'll be *fair*, don't you see? Just like you

said last night in the graveyard.'

'Right,' Mo murmured.

I very nearly sighed with relief.

Silly me.

Trust my sharp-witted twin to spot the flaw in my game plan instantly. 'But if Oldcastle *do* lose,' she said, 'you'll be stuck at Wembley by yourself, Josh. I won't be there to share the blame and the disappointment!'

'That's my problem, isn't it?'

'Josh, you're my twin. I won't let you. Besides, how are you going to keep me here – lock me up?'

'Mo,' I said, carefully. 'I've locked you up already. In a sound-proof, thief-proof, fire-proof room where nobody will disturb you till I get back after the match. See you later, Mo.' And I put down the phone.

At the foot of the stairs, I listened awhile. If Mo was shouting and kicking her door already, then I couldn't hear it.

In the lobby, I hung up our three keys – Mo's, mine and Mr Higgins's – on the rack behind the reception desk. I even remembered to disconnect the switchboard so my sister couldn't ring down for help. Then I pressed the buzzer for our landlady. Offering her a lift to her lunch date as soon as Mr Higgins got back with our car was probably my cleverest stroke of all.

Altogether, I was feeling rather pleased with myself. Or I would have if I hadn't been shaking like a leaf.

CHAPTER 10

After the Queen

Thank goodness for Freddy's rehearsals. I'd practised what I had to do so often it was completely automatic: trotting out of the tunnel, lining up on the pitch, shaking hands.

Even the atmosphere didn't affect me much. Yes, it was electric with excitement just as I'd been told to expect – with a frenzy of waving banners all round us. The noise from the crowd was even more astonishing. It rose and fell in wave after wave as if it might flood the whole arena at any moment, drowning the lot of us. But Freddy had prepared me well. Until Her

Majesty the Queen arrived.

The Queen?

At the Cup Final?

She'd made a last-minute request to be there, apparently, and especially wanted to meet me. 'Just be yourself, Josh,' was Freddy's advice. 'Treat it as something normal.'

Oh, really? Meeting the Queen is normal?

Even Freddy himself, the world's snappiest dresser, didn't look normal. His suit today was so expensive, and such a perfect fit, he must have hung it up at night on a Freddy-shaped hanger. As for Uncle Patch's famous tracksuit and carrier bag, I swear they'd both been cleaned and pressed. If the pair of them had taken this much trouble, what would the Queen herself be like?

Normal, actually.

She was dressed from top-to-toe in a smart, sky-blue outfit and was smaller than she seemed on television. Freddy nudged me towards her and I was almost paralysed with panic. What if I sneezed or fell over, or said something stupid?

'Hello, Josh,' she smiled. 'I've heard a lot about you.'

'And I've heard a lot about you,' I squeaked.

See what I mean? *Stupid.*

To my relief, she just laughed. 'Oh, but you're much more special than me, Josh. Is it true about your amazing luck?'

'Yes, ma'am.'

'Will you show me how it works?'

'Right now?' I said, uneasily.

She patted her handbag. 'Josh, I've brought a brand-new pack of playing cards – properly shuffled by my lady-in-waiting, of course. Can you pick out a Royal Flush for me?'

'In front of all these people, ma'am?'

'Is that a problem, Josh?'

I took a deep breath. 'Ma'am, may I whisper something?'

'Certainly, Josh.' Politely, she bent forward a little.

I kept my excuse as short as I could. 'It's all about *focus*, ma'am,' I hissed. 'If I don't concentrate on one thing at a time – this match, for instance – my luck might not be so strong'.

The Queen nodded at once. 'Josh, I understand perfectly. I should have thought of that for myself. Er . . . may I whisper something back to you?'

'To me, ma'am?'

'If you have a moment . . .'

If I had a moment? I was goggle-eyed, I can tell you, as Her Majesty bent forward again in front of more than ninety thousand people plus a world-wide television audience. 'Josh,' she murmured in my ear, 'if you ever get tired of football and fancy a switch to horse-racing . . . will you give me a call at the Palace?'

'You bet!' I gasped.

'I do, yes,' smiled the Queen. 'That's exactly what I had in mind!' And she winked as she moved away.

If only she'd known.

If only the Oldcastle fans had known. A little later, when Melchester United scored a quick, slick goal in the opening minute of the match, I think I was the only person at Wembley who was bothered. 'We're still settling down,' Uncle Patch remarked.

We were still settling down half-an-hour later. The truth is, we were outclassed. Melchester, with a team of eleven full internationals and three more sitting on the bench, were a little smoother, a little faster, a little sharper in every part of the field. It was like watching a goodish steeplechaser up against an absolute thoroughbred. Yet still our fans were backing us:

GOLD ARMY! GOLD ARMY! GOLD ARMY!
COME ON YOU GO-OLDS!

Also, to my dismay as I stared glumly down at my feet, they sang the chant I wanted to forget: *JOSH NOOOOO-LAN!*

I especially wanted to forget it when United scored a second goal, direct from a corner, just before half-time.

The players trooped off the pitch to howls of delight from the Melchester supporters:

EASY! EASY! EASY!

TWO–NIL TO THE NORTHERNERS . . .
COME ON YOU RE-EDS!

Our own supporters were in a state of shock. Now I had the team to face.

Wearily, I stood up. That's when Uncle Patch pulled me back. 'Hold on a sec, Josh,' he said. 'I want a word.' Even with me sitting and him standing, our eyes were more-or-less level. He cocked his snowy-white head on one side. 'Something's different, isn't it?' he remarked.

'Uncle Patch . . .'

'Yes?'

I sighed and kept quiet.

He nodded in approval. 'Well done, Josh. I was hoping you were in the mood to listen. Have you worked out what's wrong yet? It's nothing complicated, you know. Deep down, our lads are hanging about waiting for their mascot to serve up a few soft goals, gift-wrapped and delivered to our door. D'you hear what I'm saying?'

'Yes,' I mumbled.

'Now don't get me wrong. Young Mo's treated Oldcastle handsomely so far and I'm as grateful as anyone. Every team, however good it is, needs a lucky break from time to time. The trouble is, if you get to *rely* on lucky breaks the rest of your game goes to pieces and you end up with the sort of codswallop we've played this afternoon. Can you stand it, Josh, if I tell you what I really think?'

'I'll . . . I'll try.'

'Here it is, then. I like your sister a lot. She's got real grit, that kid. But, all things considered, I reckon you'd have done Oldcastle a favour if you'd left her at home today.'

'Really?' I choked.

'Yes, really. That's why I want you to stay here in the dugout while I trot along to the dressing-room to give the lads a little pep-talk. And it won't be a *pretty* pep-talk, either. Do you catch my drift?'

I nodded, dumbly.

As he turned away, he suddenly paused and looked back. 'Oh, and Josh . . .' he added.

'Yes, Uncle Patch?'

'Don't bother to wish me luck.'

CHAPTER 11

A final fluke

Don't ask me what Uncle Patch said back there in the changing room. When he returned, though, his face had the look of a good job jobbed. That's how Granny would have described it, anyway. I shot him an anxious glance. 'Can we really raise our game in the second half?' I asked.

'We'd better, Josh.'

Already he was concentrating hard.

So were Oldcastle Athletic. Somehow, at last, they'd slipped into a higher gear. After twenty minutes or so, no one was much surprised when our first goal arrived. A sharp interchange of passes between Okri, Dent and Neame led to a sliding lunge by Devon Headley who tapped the ball neatly past the Melchester keeper.

Two–one.

The ear-splitting cheer from our fans must have reached Mo, a couple of miles away, locked up in her sound-proof hotel room.

The equalizer followed only a moment later.

It was one of those fierce, instinctive drives from outside the area which seems to be travelling faster when it hits the back of the net than when it leaves the scorer's boot – in this case, Ben Vronsky's.

Two–all.

The Oldcastle supporters went wild. Soon, the uproar from every foot-stomping, scarf-waving, up-and-down-jumping body in the stadium had switched to the anthem every underdog loves to hear:

YOU'RE NOT SINGING
YOU'RE NOT SINGING
YOU'RE NOT SINGING ANY MORE!
YOU'RE NOT SI-I-I-NG-ING ANY MORE!

Uncle Patch gave a chuckle. 'Now the fun really begins . . .'

'What?'

'Son, both sides will run themselves into the ground after this – them to save face, us because we believe in ourselves again. We're in for a cracker of a climax!' He was right about that.

People still talk about the closing stages of the match. 'A privilege to be there,' they say. 'Showpiece soccer at its best – excellence with *attitude*!'

We hit the crossbar twice, plus a post. They hit both our posts plus the crossbar. For skill, and fitness and teamwork, there wasn't a jot of difference between the two sides. 'How long can they keep up this pace?' exclaimed Uncle Patch. He meant Melchester as much as Oldcastle.

Then came the breakthrough.

It happened in the last minute as usual. By now I should've been used to this. The long swerving pass looked utterly harmless to me . . . at any rate while the ball was in the air. Once it struck the turf, though, it skidded awkwardly in the worst bounce of the match. No one, surely, could blame our sweeper, Mickey Rice, when it hit him somewhere below the elbow. 'Penalty!' snapped Uncle Patch straightaway.

'It was an accident!' I protested.

'Was it, Josh? Even Mickey might have doubts about that. Besides, there's no point in arguing. The referee's pointing to the spot. This could be the decider.' His voice was amazingly calm.

Me, I could barely breathe let alone talk. This was the decider all right . . . not just of the match but also of our team's future. If Melchester scored now, we were probably finished. Who remembers Cup-losers, after all? But suppose Racer Carr made a save?

That would bring extra-time – another half-hour in which anything could happen. Having got ourselves off the hook so spectacularly, weren't we bound to have the advantage?

RACER! RACER! RACER! RACER! RACER!

Our captain lifted a hand to the crowd then settled himself in the goal-mouth. Their spot-kick specialist began his run-up . . . at which point, for me, everything went into slow-motion.

THWACK!

Like a movie screened frame-by-frame, the ball moved lazily to the right as Racer, guessing wrongly, moved left . . . except not quite left since he corrected himself in the nick of time.

His glove made just enough contact to nudge the ball up . . . up . . . and up towards the join of post and crossbar.

THUD!

The whole goal shuddered as the ball ricocheted safely back into play.

Almost. As he recovered, Racer couldn't help clipping the ball with his heel . . . and it rolled gently, ever so gently, across our goal-line into the net.

It was the flukiest penalty ever scored.

But it was perfectly legal: Melchester United three, Oldcastle Athletic two. Almost immediately, the referee turned half the stadium to stone by blowing his whistle. We'd been beaten by a piece of sheer . . . sheer . . .

I couldn't bring myself to say the word. I felt terrible. Oldcastle had lost and it was all my fault. Then everything became a bit dream-like. It was a good thing Freddy had made us rehearse so much. The whole rigmarole of collecting our runner's up medals, of applauding Melchester's lap of honour, of giving interviews to the press without – on Uncle Patch's strict instructions – mentioning the phrase 'we woz robbed' even once, managed to keep us more or less dignified. What amazed me was the friendliness of Oldcastle's players when I tried to say sorry. 'Sorry?' said Racer. 'Don't be daft, Josh. None of the lads blame you for what happened.'

'But I let you down, didn't I?'

'How d'you work that out? Luck's luck, after

all – no one's got a monopoly on the stuff. Besides, haven't you already done us proud this season?'

When the team gave me three cheers, I felt awful.

Uncle Patch made me feel even worse. 'Brace up, son,' he grinned at me. 'It's not the end of the world, you know.'

'Tell that to Freddy Wedge,' I said bitterly.

'He's already doing the telling himself, Josh. To anyone who'll listen . . . radio, TV, the newspapers. He's given them the perfect soundbite as well: THE LOSERS WHO BECAME A LEGEND. Classy, eh? I'd rate it above THE LUCKIEST WINNERS IN HISTORY any day of the week.'

'Would you?'

'Yes,' said Uncle Patch firmly. 'I would.' I left him surrounded by reporters.

Gran would be waiting, I knew. So would Dustin and Sheena – probably hopping up and down beside her, crazy with questions. I just couldn't face them, not yet. Instead, I slipped back up the tunnel and out onto the pitch.

Already the stadium was three-quarters empty but it still looked pretty impressive to me. High above, the oval of sky framed by the surrounding grandstands had an early-summer blueness . . . and I could see swallows dipping their wings in and out of the shadowy roofspace.

It was lovely, yes.

And right now I hated the sight of it. Tearfully, I spread both my arms and let rip

with an agonized howl. 'They lost!' I screeched. 'They lost the most important match in the club's history! And it was only luck that did it!'

'Exactly,' came a voice I recognized at once.

'You?' I gasped, whirling round.

'There's no need to look so surprised, Josh. Haven't you heard of after-sales service?'

And out of the dug-out stepped the peanut seller.

CHAPTER 12

Peanuts forever!

He was just as I remembered him. In fact, with his stooping shoulders and grainy, puckered-up face, he looked a bit like a peanut himself. 'Congratulations, Josh!' he greeted me. 'I've seen for myself what you've done with your luck – or your sister's luck, rather.'

'Wait,' I mumbled. 'I can explain . . .'

'Explain what, Josh?'

The peanut seller smacked his lips. 'It's a brilliant result for Oldcastle, you know. The best result possible, I'd say.'

I stared at him, blankly. Had he been

watching the same match as me?

He gave me a sideways, peanutty smile. 'Don't you get it, Josh? Just when Oldcastle's run of good luck was beginning to get up people's noses, along comes some so-called "bad" luck to win back their sympathy. Next season, Oldcastle Athletic will be the most popular team in the whole of the Premier League!'

'But what about The Canyon of the Future?'

'What about it? Thanks to that dodgy penalty, it's a certainty now – everyone will be falling over themselves to pour money into Freddy's project. Your sister's the best thing that ever happened to Oldcastle.'

If only I could have believed it. Miserably, I shook my head. 'But she wasn't even here,' I groaned.

'What?'

'Mo wasn't here.'

'Not here, Josh? At Wembley, you mean?'

'I locked her in her room back at the hotel. I nobbled her, you see, so she wouldn't have to be the Multi-Million-Pound Mascot any more.'

The peanut seller's eyes twinkled. Then he started to laugh. It wasn't a small laugh, either. What came out was a shoulder-shaking, belly-slapping guffaw that echoed along the terraces

in a series of spluttery, hiccupy hoots. 'You nobbled the luckiest kid alive?' he snorted. 'By locking her in her hotel room?'

'Yes,' I said, stiffly. 'I did.'

'Bless me, Josh. Did you really think you could keep her there? Imagine a broken catch on a window, say . . . and a handy drainpipe outside reaching right down to the ground. Any chance of those in your opinion?'

'They're possible, yes . . .'

'Possible, Josh? Forget *possible*. It's downright definite for a kid like Mo. If she'd made up her mind to come, nothing could stop her getting here. Why, it wouldn't even have worked if you'd disconnected the hotel switchboard!'

That's when the penny dropped. Only one person could have told him such a thing. 'OK, mister,' I said. 'You can stop all your teasing. Where is Mo, then?'

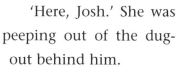

'Here, Josh.' She was peeping out of the dug-out behind him.

Her face-paint had gone a bit streaky by now. Also her team-strip was as rumpled as you'd expect after such a hectic afternoon. My twin sister looked . . . well, she looked rather like me, I suppose. 'When did you arrive?' I asked her.

'Just after the Queen, Josh. A mascot has to be somewhere in the stadium, after all. Otherwise the luck won't happen.'

I felt dizzy with relief. 'So the peanut seller's right. Oldcastle really did get the best possible result . . .'

'Of course they did. All I needed to do was rely on the Peanut. It was never going to let us down, Josh, in any way, shape or form. Once I remembered that, and realized there was nothing to worry about, I rushed here as fast as I could. Isn't it wonderful? I gave the team just the sort of luck they needed . . . and my days as their mascot are over!'

'But aren't you still mega-lucky?'

'Oh, yes . . .' Mo's smile was the happiest I've ever seen.

It was a green-and-gold smile, too, since she'd even painted her teeth in Oldcastle's colours.

From under her arm she took the battered and much-thumbed paperback which she seemed to carry everywhere these days. She was gazing across the famous Wembley turf as she leafed through its pages. 'You know what this is, Josh?' she said over her shoulder.

'Some sort of science book, isn't it?'

'Actually it's about volcanoes and tidal-waves, droughts and hurricanes,' said Mo. 'All the disasters which bring so much bad luck to the world. That's what I'm going to study after

I leave school, Josh. In an utterly scientific way, of course. So no one will ever guess I've got a little bit of extra . . . well, let's say "help". Every scientist needs a dollop of that to solve a problem. Who knows, maybe I can make it possible for every country in the world to grow Peanuts of Power!' Her face seemed to glow at the thought.

So did mine, probably.

You see, I was pretty sure she could do it. Couldn't the Multi-Million-Pound Mascot do pretty nearly anything she chose provided she had what Uncle Patch called 'real grit'?

Still beaming, I turned back to the dug-out. 'Hey, Mr Peanut-Seller,' I laughed.'What do you think of Mo's plan?' But he'd already vanished.

And he stayed vanished however hard Mo and I looked in that huge, rambling, football-infested arena. In the end, we simply shrugged and gave up the search. Somehow, we knew already that we'd never see him again. 'Does that matter, Josh?' asked Mo, anxiously.

'It doesn't matter a bit,' I told her. 'Like

everything else that's happened today, it's exactly as it should be.'

'You really think so?'

'Trust me, Mo.' Of course, I grinned as I said it.

My sister grinned, too, as she slipped her hand in mine and we set off across the almost deserted stadium to meet Gran, Dustin and Sheena. By now, we realized, they'd be fizzing with rage at how long we'd kept them hanging about. Mo and I were in deep, deep trouble . . . unless, that is, we had a stroke of you know what.

About the author

I've written more than
fifty books for children,
including *Sharks* – also
for OUP. Few of them
have given me as much
fun as *The Multi-Million-
Pound Mascot*, though.

Partly this is because
I'm a twin myself, just like Josh, but mostly
because I'm a life-long supporter of Charlton
Athletic Football Club in South London. So are
my two daughters, Kate and Ellie. We never
miss a home match – though they sit near the
goal and I prefer the half-way line.

  We always cheer Charlton's mascots
especially loudly even though there's never
been one quite like Mo in my story!

Other Treetops books in this set include:
Snowblind   Paul Stewart
Lolly Woe   Anna Perera
One Girl School   Jon Blake
My Guinea-Pig is Innocent   Margaret McAllister
The War Monkey   Claire Funge

Also available in packs:
Stage 16 pack G   0 19 919384 3
Stage 16 class pack G   0 19 919385 1

Treetops books at this level include:
Melleron's Monsters   Douglas Hill
Melleron's Magic   Douglas Hill
Swivel-Head   Susan Gates
Sister Ella   Pippa Goodhart
Carnival   Julie Sykes
In the Shadow of the Striker   David Clayton

Also available in packs:
Stage 16 pack E   0 19 919275 8
Stage 16 class pack E   0 19 919276 6